Ralph Miller
2

THE ONE AND ONLY SECOND

AUTOBIOGRAPHY

THE DOG WH

LANDMARK EDITIONS, INC.
Kansas City, Missouri

f RALPH MILLER

'NEW HE WAS A BOY

ANOTHER
HILARIOUS THRILLER
WRITTEN AND ILLUSTRATED BY
DAVID MELTON

Third Printing

COPYRIGHT © 1983 and 1986   David Melton

Jacket and book design by David Melton

Library of Congress Cataloging in Publication Data

Melton, David.
   The one and only second autobiography of Ralph Miller, the dog who knew he was a boy.

   Summary: The further adventures of Ralph Miller, who begins to wonder if life wouldn't have been easier if he had been content to live it as a dog, since he looks so much like one.
   [1. Dogs—Fiction]   I. Title.
[PZ7.M51640nd   1986]   [Fic]   86-27556
ISBN 0-933849-31-1 (LIB.BDG.)
ISBN 0-933849-06-0 (pbk.)

Landmark Editions, Inc.
1420 Kansas Avenue
Kansas City, Missouri 64127

Printed in the United States of America

To
James and Peggy Bane

INTRODUCTION

From the start, let me make a few things perfectly clear. I had reservations about writing my first autobiography and I certainly never intended to write a second. But during the last years I have received so many letters from readers and so many exciting things have happened to me since the first book was published, I had little choice but to sit down at the typewriter once again.

It seems there is still the question in the minds of many—am I a dog who talks and writes like a boy, or am I really a boy who happens to look like a dog? Of course, I know the truth and I have tried to tell it. Those who believe what I write are convinced and those who don't aren't. And there's nothing I can do about that.

If anyone should ask what you think, I hope you reply, "Ralph Miller is alive and well and living in Prairie Village." If no one asks, who cares?

But for now, don't bother your head with such thoughts. Just sit back, relax and enjoy this book—for the action is about to begin!

Ralph Miller

Josie - locked behind bars.

TRAPPED AGAIN

Have you ever noticed that almost nothing ever turns out the way you plan? Well, I have.

Plan a picnic — it starts to rain.

Plan a skiing trip — it won't snow.

Try to plan your life — those plans crumble before your eyes.

Plans are easy to make — it's those dead ends, those turns of fate, that suddenly appear and cause the trouble. They are the spoilers of plans and the killers of dreams. They provide the times that try men's souls. YUCK!

For instance, consider my plan — it was simple enough. Because people were unable to accept Josie and me as the persons we really are, we decided to go into the mountains and I would become a famous author. No reason why that wouldn't work. All we needed was some remote mountain and a typewriter.

"Come on, Josie," I had said as we left my parents' home that night. "We have a long way to go."

Let me tell you something — unless you are a flea carrying a brick on your back, six blocks is not a very long way to go. And that's as far as we had traveled — less than six blocks — when three police cars surrounded us and came to a screeching halt. We were immediately grabbed in the arms of the law. They clamped leather muzzles tight over our heads — holding our mouths shut. We had no chance to complain or explain.

One of the policemen checked Josie's tags and said excitedly, "She's the one!"

Then, they pushed us into the back seat of one of the squad cars and began talking about how they were going to split up the reward. The two in the front seat laughed and joked about how they were going to spend the money. The siren squealed as the car sped into the night.

All I could see through the wire mesh separating the front seat from the back was a rifle strapped above the windshield. Josie was next to me, crouched down, shivering with fright. I knew I must have looked the same.

Since we had done nothing wrong, I tried to tell myself that everything would be all right. These men were police officers who were paid to protect innocent people. But all their talk of reward and money signaled danger.

When the squad car pulled in front of the police station, it came to an abrupt stop. They snatched Josie and me from the back seat and rushed into the brick building.

"We got her," called out the first officer.

"Get that guy on the phone," the chief ordered.

The sergeant hurried to the phone and dialed a number.

While Josie was held captive in a cell in the squad room, I was taken to a smaller room and the door was shut and locked. I jumped up in a chair and looked through the window that separated me from the squad room. All their attention was centered on Josie. The chief checked her tags for himself and shook hands with the arresting officers. Then came more talk of reward money.

"I'm in for a share, too," the chief informed the men, "and since I'm the chief, I get 50 percent."

"Hey, that's not fair. We caught her," the officers argued.

"Okay, we'll split it three ways," the chief finally agreed.

As they greedily divided up her future, Josie shivered and looked over at me. She no longer expected help — there was only quiet despair in her eyes.

During the next half hour, the officers walked back and forth to the front door, eagerly looking outside for something — or someone. But who? Or what? I wondered. And then, I heard it — "Hmm-mmmmmmmmmmmmmmmmmmmmmmmmmmmmm" — that well-tuned engine, every cylinder perfectly ground. The mysterious black sedan pulled up in front of the station and stopped.

I could hear the car doors open and shut. I heard two men coming up the steps. I knew who they were — we had met before. The fat one was the first to enter the room. The skinny one followed close behind.

"There she is!" said the skinny one, pointing.

"Why yes, there's our little darlin'," cooed the fat one in false, friendly tones. "Why we've been worried sick. We was scared she was hit by a car or lost for good."

Fat One   Skinny One

"Are you the owner of the dog?" the chief asked.

"Not exactly," gruffed the fat one. "She belongs to our boss."

"Then why isn't he here?" asked the chief.

The fat one shook his head sadly. "Poor man is beside himself with worry and grief. We had to call the doctor for tranquilizers."

"Do you have proof of ownership?" the Chief wanted to know.

"We have this bill of sale," said the skinny one, taking a slip of paper from his shirt pocket.

"And," the fat one declared, holding out a handful of greenbacks, "this five thousand dollars reward money."

Once the officers saw the money, they had no interest in examining the bill of sale. The chief quickly took the money and began counting it — one hundred, two hundred, three hundred, four — all the way up to five thousand dollars.

"There's your dog," said the chief, pointing to Josie.

She tried to growl, but the muzzle muffled her sounds. The fat one and the skinny one grabbed her and held her tight.

"She doesn't seem too pleased to see you," noticed one of the officers.

"She's a one-owner dog," the fat one replied.

"Yeh," the skinny one said. "She's the boss's pet."

"She adores him," the fat one lied.

And they carried Josie from the room, out the front door, and to the car. I heard the engine start, the low hmmmmmmmmmmmmmmmmmmmmmm, as it sped into the night.

Josie was gone.

I spent a long and lonely night in jail. At about nine o'clock the next morning, I heard my father's voice and when I looked through the window, I saw him talking with the police chief. I heard the chief tell him there was a leash law in Prairie Village and, if they ever found me loose on the streets again, that he would have to pay a fine. Dad promised it would not happen again.

When the door was unlocked, Dad came into the room and bent down. He took the muzzle off my face, picked me up, and carried me outside.

"They took Josie," I finally said.

"I know," he replied.

2

LET ME BE AND BE GONE!

I don't know about you, but I think growing up is rough. Throughout the world, millions of babies are born, they get to be children for a while, then they have to grow up and become adults. Wouldn't you think by now we would have developed a better system? I do.

Philosophers often maintain that we learn from our trials and errors. That may be true. But I sometimes wonder — what's the point? It seems that no sooner do I learn from one trial and think I'm on my way to becoming a successful person, than I'm faced with another trial. I am beginning to feel that my life is nothing but a long list of checks and balances. But there doesn't seem to be any grand total.

My father says I was born with a creative spirit. When he says this, there is a sense of pride in his voice — as if this creative spirit is something magical and wonderful. I suppose it is. But this creative spirit, with all its wonders, also gets me into a lot of trouble!

When I look back on my life, it appears to me that things might have been easier. Because of my paws, tail, and furry face, I could have acted as if I was a dog. Maybe I should have done that. It wasn't such a bad life. There was always food in the bowl and plenty of fresh water. I had a nice family. And I was often petted.

Okay, every so often, I had to fetch a stick or bring in the evening paper. But if I wanted attention, all I had to do was wiggle my tail or bark at the mailman.

I think, at first, I only saw the advantages of being a boy and never noticed the consequences. I saw that Jeff and Tim were allowed to go to school and make many of their own decisions. They could decide if they wanted to play football or read a book or visit friends or go to a movie. I didn't understand that these advantages also brought certain responsibilities — such as homework, washing dishes, raking leaves, mowing the yard, and carrying out the trash.

If only I could have been content to allow other people to open the door for me, things might have been less complicated. But no, not me, not Ralph Miller! I couldn't leave well enough alone. I had to see how the doorknob worked. I had to learn how to turn it myself and pull the door open.

And then I couldn't be satisfied having thoughts of my own and keeping them to myself. Oh no, I had to open my big mouth and learn to talk.

And then I couldn't just stay at home and talk to the members of my family. No, I had to go to school and show off all my skills and talents. And where did this creative spirit lead me? It led me straight into the trunk of the mysterious black sedan with the hmmmmmm engine. It led me into the hands of the fat one and the skinny one and, worst of all, into the greedy clutches of the Boss. It led me to quick capture and narrow escape, running across empty fields and down dark alleys.

Still, of course, it led me to Josie — beautiful Josie — held prisoner by the Boss. I freed her once, but now she is his prisoner again.

The truth about creativity is this: if you paint with your fingers, you can wind up with messy paws.

The worst part about following one's creative spirit is that every road doesn't lead to instant success. Some lead to failure. And when we fail, we feel sorry for ourselves. Which is all right—as long as you don't let it get you down. As you have probably guessed, I was feeling pretty sorry for myself. And I was letting it get me down. Some people say that misery loves company. Not mine — my misery wanted to be left alone. All I wanted to do was roll over and play dead.

But they wouldn't leave me alone. Tim would walk into my room and say, "Cheer up, Ralph. Things aren't as bad as they seem."

It took every bit of restraint I could muster not to punch him in the nose.

And Mother would say, "Ralph, try to look on the bright side. You are alive and safe at home."

"Being alive and safe isn't everything. I'm also very miserable," I told her.

And then one evening, I was in my room — the draperies were closed. I was lying on my bed — half asleep, half awake, half thinking, and half not thinking — when my father knocked on the door and stepped inside, I knew what was coming — more words of patient understanding and more words of sympathy — or so I thought.

Dad

Mom

"What are you doing in here?" he wanted to know.

"Nothing," I answered slowly, heaving a long sigh.

"That's what I thought. Get up and carry out the

trash," he ordered. "We're tired of waiting on you. We have responsibilities in this family and so do you!"

I wondered what had happened to the words of sympathy.

"All right," I moaned. "Just give me a few minutes."

"Right now!" Dad demanded. "You've felt sorry for yourself long enough. Get up!"

That last "get up" told me patient understanding was gone too. I rolled over and climbed out of bed.

"Look," I told him. "I don't know whether you've noticed or not, but I'm going through a bad time."

"Noticed!" he exclaimed. "Ever since you came home, you've done nothing but walk around with your tail between your legs, sighing, 'Woe is me.' I thought you were a boy — not some sniffling pup."

"Is this the beginning of one of your 'life is tough' speeches?" I quipped bitterly.

"You listen to me, Ralph Miller," he said firmly. "Do you think you're the only one in the world who has ever failed? Well, welcome to the club. A man is not measured by how much he succeeds; his true measure is how he overcomes failure."

"I'm not a man," I replied. "I'm a boy."

"And is that what you intend to be for the rest of your life?" he inquired. "Or are you ever going to grow up?"

"How does carrying out the trash make me any more of a man?" I wanted to know.

"It doesn't," he said, "but it takes up the time in between."

"I don't appreciate your point of view," I told him.

"How would you appreciate a smack on your rear end?" he asked.

"Not much," I snapped. "I'm not into physical violence."

"And I'm not into self-pity," he replied.

"But don't you realize it's my fault that Josie was caught and returned to the Boss? She's probably locked in some dark room right now, guarded by the fat one and the skinny one. She's there because I failed to protect her."

"Nonsense," Dad insisted. "You did everything you could. Josie being captured by the police and turned over to the Boss was not because you failed her. Your failure is sitting here in your room and giving up."

"But I don't know what to do or where to start,"
I admitted.

"You start by carrying out the trash," he said
flatly.

It was apparent Dad was not going to forget
about the trash.

"Yes, sir," I said grumpily and stalked out of the
room.

I entered the living room. There sat Jeff and Tim
— square eyeballs glued to the TV set — playing
Pac-Man.

Tim

Jeff

"Gotcha," said Tim, moving the control.
"Gotcha back," Jeff yelled back.
I thought surely one of them would show some

compassion for me and offer to take out the trash. No way. Traitors!

I walked into the kitchen. Maybe Mother would offer to help. But she didn't even turn around. So I carried the trash outside — but I didn't feel any better for having done it.

The next day, I raked the leaves in the yard and stuffed them into bags — but I didn't feel any better.

I even opened the curtains in my room and stopped sitting in the dark — but that didn't make me feel any better either.

Then it occurred to me that I would never feel any better until I quit thinking about myself. I was being selfish, thinking only about how *I* felt, never considering poor trapped Josie. I knew I had to find a way to rescue Josie. I would never feel better until Josie was free and the Boss and his worthless thugs were put away for good. But how could I do this, I wondered. I didn't know, but I was determined to try!

SWITCHING TRACKS

Of course, Dad was right. I had wrapped myself up in a cocoon of self-pity. Not only had I removed myself from the members of my family, but I had ignored friends and acquaintances. I decided it was time to change that. I ran across the yard and through the gate. The chill of early winter was in the air. I hurried to the doghouse, and knocked on the door.

Bruno slowly edged his head out the doorway

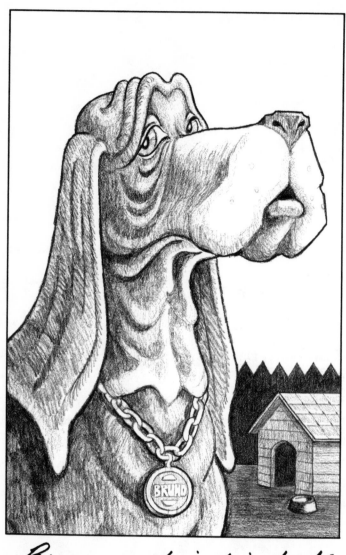

Bruno - a friend indeed!

and looked at me with sleepy eyes.

"Is it morning or afternoon?" he yawned.

"Morning," I answered.

"Good," he said. "Then I haven't missed my afternoon nap."

"Aren't you feeling well?" I asked.

"Just old age," he replied, stretching his front legs slowly back and forth. "Got a touch of arthritis in my shoulder. That cold wind doesn't help."

"I'm sorry you are ill," I said.

"Who told you that?" he wanted to know. "I'm fit as a fiddle. I bet it was that loudmouth Fifi who filled your head with such nonsense."

"I haven't seen Fifi," I replied.

"Lucky you," he said clicking his teeth. "She's always showing off her blue ribbons and yak, yak, yaking."

"That's Fifi, all right," I mused.

"Show dogs are such a nuisance," Bruno remarked. "Poor things, all they have is their looks and when those start to go it's downhill all the way."

"But Fifi was always a winner," I said.

"She *was*. Second place is the best she can do

anymore," he whispered. "The competition is too fierce. All the young poodles have fluffier coats, straighter legs, and shinier teeth."

"Poor Fifi," I sighed, thinking it over.

"Sorry about Josie," Bruno said suddenly.

The wind suddenly felt colder.

"It was a real shock," I admitted.

"You talkers have a rough row to hoe," Bruno said thoughtfully. "I tried to warn you."

"I know," I admitted, "but I was too stubborn to listen."

"You were determined," Bruno replied. "You tried to improve yourself and you did."

"Maybe it was just pride," I told him. "Perhaps I'm more like Fifi than I like to admit."

"I don't think so," Bruno said. "The quest for knowledge and showing off are two different things."

"But mine is only a shallow achievement," I told him. "Oh, I can speak the language of people. I can read, write, and solve algebraic equations, but they will never accept me as one of them."

"Your family has," Bruno said.

"Yes," I agreed. "They're wonderful people. And there are a few others who are willing to accept new ideas. But not many."

"I'm afraid you are right," Bruno sighed. "My owner is a nice man, but he would never understand. One day, after he read the newspaper article about you going to school, he came out to the yard, held up the picture and laughed, 'Why don't you do something like this, Bruno?' I almost said, 'I can, you old fool,' but I didn't. He would have died on the spot."

"You didn't tell me you could talk, too!" I exclaimed.

"Nothing to brag about. Only a few words here and there," he admitted.

"But why didn't you learn more?"

"No ambition, I guess," he shrugged. "Never could figure out what I would do with it except, maybe, work in a circus. But that kind of life has never appealed to me."

"Perhaps that's where I'll end up," I said gloomily. "Hurry, hurry, hurry, come one, come all. See the freaks, see the clowns. See Ralph Miller, the talking dog. He walks, he talks. He spouts out tongue-twisting riddles and mind-boggling nerds of nonsense."

"Don't belittle yourself, Ralph," Bruno scolded.

"I expect better than that from you."

"That's just the trouble, everybody expects more from me," I complained. "My father expects me to seek my fullest potential. My mother wants me to do great things. And even Josie. . ." I stopped for a moment. "I don't know what Josie expected, except that I would keep her safe from the Boss and the fat one and the skinny one. Looks like she expected too much. With a muzzle lashed over my mouth, I couldn't talk our way out of that one."

"You've just been sidetracked," Bruno told me.

"I've been derailed," I concluded.

"Maybe it's time for you to review your goals," he suggested.

"I don't have any goals now," I told him. "I was going to be a writer — funny stories and witty sayings. I pictured myself as some kind of furry Will Rogers, but I don't feel like writing jokes and poking fun now."

"What do you feel?" Bruno asked.

"I feel nothing but rage," I confessed. "I'm tired of people being judged by the way they look. I see pups who are eager to learn but treated like dogs. Why can't people see that we are all the same — only different?"

"That's what you should write," Bruno said matter-of-factly.

"But I have to find Josie," I insisted.

"I may be able to help, Ralph," Bruno said. "I used to know a German shepherd who worked with the detective squad in Kansas City. Haven't seen him for years, but I heard he retired a few months back. I'll try to get in touch with him and see if he will help."

"Is he a good detective?" I wanted to know.

"The *best*," Bruno replied without blinking an eye.

"Great!" I exclaimed. "Let's get him now."

"It isn't quite that simple," Bruno told me. "Since his retirement, I hear he's been on the skids — holed up on the East Side — a tough part of town."

"We'll go in and bring him out," I said excitedly.

"No one goes into the East Side without an invitation and lives to tell about it," Bruno pointed out. "And no one brings Daschell out of anyplace, unless he wants out. I think I can get a message in. If Daschell can get out, he'll come. He owes me one."

I was curious as to why Daschell owned Bruno a

favor — but one look at Bruno's tightly-clenched jaw and I realized I shouldn't ask. So, I didn't.

"Now then," Bruno said. "I have my job and you have yours."

I had no doubt what he meant — I was to leave the detective business to Bruno and I was to start writing!

4

GETTING STARTED

When I placed a sheet of paper in the typewriter and centered it, the white space seemed to overpower my words and thoughts. I stared at the keys of the typewriter. They were no help. "Leave us alone," they seemed to say. "Take your ideas somewhere else. Go out in the street and play."

I broke out in a cold sweat. I was stopped before I began. I began to suspect that becoming a writer might not be as easy as I had thought.

Then, I remembered that only a few blocks from our house, there lived a writer. He'd had more than twenty books published. I had read a couple of them and thought they were pretty good. I reached for the telephone book — not really thinking his name would be included because everyone knows famous authors have unlisted telephone numbers.

I made a note to myself: Get an unlisted number.

My eyes followed my paw down the list of M's and to my surprise, I found his name — **David Melton** — and next to his name was a number. So much for famous writers, I thought — but decided to call him anyway.

I dialed the number. I probably won't get past his secretary. Everyone knows famous authors never answer their own phones. They have private secretaries to handle their calls and make appointments.

I made another note to myself: Get a private secretary.

The phone rang several times and then a man's voice answered, "Hello."

"May I speak to Mr. Melton, please?" I asked.

"This is he," the voice replied.

"Are you the David Melton who is the writer?"

"Yes," he said.

"My name is Ralph Miller," I told him, "and I am writing a book."

"How many pages have you written?" Mr. Melton inquired.

"Well, none yet," I admitted.

"Then, you aren't *writing* a book," he said. "You're just thinking about it."

"But I have the paper in the typewriter," I insisted.

"So, what can I do for you?" he asked.

"How do I start?" I suddenly blurted out.

There was a long pause and then he spoke again.

"Did you ever hear how Winston Churchill began painting?" he asked.

"No."

"Well, he started late in life," Mr. Melton told me. "Sir Winston had already been secretary of the British Navy, had served terms in the House of Parliament and was known throughout the world. Anyway, he had always had an urge to paint and he decided not to put it off any longer. So, he had his secretary make a trip to the local art store and purchase the finest oil paints, the best brushes, an easel, a palette, and the largest canvas he could find."

"Does this have anything to do with writing?" I asked impatiently.

"It has everything to do with writing, Mr. Miller," replied Mr. Melton emphatically.

"Sorry," I said. "I'm sometimes all mouth. But if you will continue, I promise to be all ears."

"All right," he said. "At any rate, Sir Winston set up his easel on the lawn of his country estate. He secured the canvas to the front. He remembered having learned in school that the three primary colors are red, yellow, and blue, so he opened the tubes of paint and squeezed out a portion of each on his palette. He looked at the large rectangle of white canvas that was set before him and he was suddenly struck with the feeling of stark terror."

"That's exactly what happened to me," I interrupted.

"Of course, it did," Mr. Melton said. "It happens to me every time I start a new book or a new chapter."

"What did Mr. Churchill do?" I asked.

"For more than an hour, he didn't do anything but sit and look at the canvas — which he later said had quite clearly and completely overwhelmed him."

"Then what happened?" I urged.

"Well," Mr. Melton continued. "That afternoon, Mrs. Churchill was having friends in for tea and, as one of the guests arrived, she happened to notice Sir Winston on the lawn. Instead of going into the house, she walked across to where he was sitting. 'I say, Winnie,' she said. 'What do you think you are doing?' Sir Winston was quite annoyed and growled back, 'I'm painting. Can't you see?'

"The lady looked at the empty canvas and retorted, 'That's utter nonsense.' Without saying another word, she took the palette from his hand, swirled a brush through the globs of blue and red and yellow, mixing them all together into a brownish mess. Raising the brush to the canvas, she made several ugly marks across the surface. Then, she handed the palette back to the astonished Mr. Churchill and walked toward the house. Sir Winston said if he had not been so surprised he might have punched her in the nose or at least tripped her."

"But what did he do then?" I asked laughing.

"He looked up at the canvas and, when he saw the paint dripping down its surface, Sir Winston realized the woman had done him a great favor,"

Mr. Melton said. "She had done what he had been afraid to attempt. She had destroyed the power of the white. Sir Winston realized there was now no way he could make the canvas look worse. Anything he might do would only improve its appearance. He was no longer afraid, and he began to paint."

"But what does that have to do with writing?" I asked.

"Ralph, if I were in your room at this moment," Mr. Melton replied, "I would make large marks on your paper and destroy the power of the white. Since I am not there, you must have the courage to do it yourself. Of course, your marks will be letters and words. It makes little difference what those first words say. The important thing is that, as quickly as possible, you should type something — anything! You must destroy the power of the white."

"I will," I promised. "May I ask you one other question?"

"What is it?"

"Do you ever carry out the trash?" I inquired.

"Of course," Mr. Melton replied.

I thanked him for his help, hung up the phone,

and made another note to myself: Writers are people too.

I did exactly as Mr. Melton had instructed. I immediately began destroying the power of the white paper. I started typing the first words that came into my mind — not worrying about sentences or paragraphs — but concentrating on thoughts and ideas.

I began to learn a lot about writing and books. I soon realized that a book is nothing but a patchwork of statements. A writer doesn't have to start at the beginning — he can write part of the middle, work on the ending, and come back to the beginning. The reader doesn't care which part was written first or second or even last. The writer is free to attack the work from any direction he chooses.

Why didn't someone tell me that writing is fun? Everyone had told me it was hard work. How little they know. Writing isn't dull or drab — it's the most exciting game in town. It's like playing mental ping pong with the paper. You hit an idea to the paper and then the paper smacks another idea right back at you. It's certainly more fun than playing Pac-Man because you aren't competing with some programmed game—you are competing with yourself, one on one. And if you don't like the rules, you can put another piece of paper into the typewriter and change them.

If everyone knew how much fun writing really is, television sets would be turned off by the millions and the sound of typewriters rat-a-tat-tatting would be heard throughout the land.

Soon, I became so engrossed in my work that I resented any interruption. When Mother told me dinner was ready, I was annoyed. When Dad stepped into the room and asked, "How's it going?" I wished he would leave me alone. If Jeff or Tim stepped in, I wanted to tell them to eat worms.

I wished I had gone to that mountaintop and found a typewriter. There, the only interruptions I would have had to endure would have been the muted sounds of crickets or distant thunder.

And then, suddenly, I realized that while I had been writing I had even forgotten about Josie. And I felt ashamed.

I asked Bruno if he had received any word from the detective.

"Not yet," Bruno replied, "but we're getting closer. I talked to a guy who saw him the other day. The word is out that I'm trying to reach Daschell.

The message will finally get through. Be patient," Bruno advised.

I tried to be patient. I really tried.

Then one night, as I lay in bed, I heard voices coming from the back of our yard. I climbed out of bed and went to the window. I could see figures moving by the bushes. At first, I couldn't tell who they were. Then, I recognized the slow loping stride of my friend, Bruno, and I could see there were at least two others with him. One was a bulldog — as tough and rough as any I had ever met. The other one was a little chihuahua. His coat was slick with grease and he walked with a nervous limp.

Their conversation was short. Soon, the bulldog and the chihuahua nodded their heads in agreement and ran down the alley. After they had gone, I watched as Bruno moved his aching shoulder back and forth. His arthritis had flared up again. I could tell he was in pain. Venturing out in the night air must surely make it worse. Bruno — such a loyal and trustworthy person — I thought, *I* owe you one, too, old friend.

TEA AND MILK BONE

The invitation arrived by mail. Before I opened it, I knew who had sent it. The embossed blue ribbon on the back flap and the simple monogram FF were ample clues. But the fine print below which stated, "International Champion," left no doubt — it was **Fifi!**

What did *she* want, I wondered.

I opened the envelope and removed the card. It read:

Miss Fifi
International Champion of Poodles
1978, '79, '80, & '81
requests the honor of your presence
Tuesday afternoon, October 6
at 2:00 p.m.
for tea and milk bone
RSVP

Just like Fifi, I thought. A simple telephone call would have been sufficient. But no, not Fifi. She sends an engraved invitation. I started to sit down and type a snappy reply stating, "Can't make it, honey. See you later." Such an answer would have served her right. But then, I noticed that the International Champion of 1982 was not listed on the card. It had not been overlooked. I knew then — that honor must have been awarded to someone else. Poor Fifi — second place! So, of course, I wrote a note saying I would be pleased to have tea and milk bone with her ladyship.

On Tuesday afternoon, I made a point of arriving at her front door at precisely 2:00 in the afternoon. Although Fifi was often late, she demanded punctuality in others. I rang the doorbell and waited. The butler, starched from his shoelaces to his British accent, opened the door and peered down at me.

"Yes?" he said with a sniff.

"Please tell Fifi that Ralph Miller is here," I said.

"Please come in," he said sniffing again.

As I entered the hall, I couldn't help but notice the white marble statue of Fifi which stood like a monument before me. It had been chiseled by a famous Italian artist.

"I will tell *Miss* Fifi you have arrived," the butler said and, giving a short but polite bow, he left the drawing room.

There was splendor everywhere — plush draperies, handcarved furniture — French Provincial of course. And over the fireplace, an oil portrait of the grand champion herself. On the opposite wall were photographs of Fifi and her many triumphs. There were ribbons of red and blue and gold, and silver trophies as well — nothing gaudy but leaving no doubt that Miss Fifi was no common pooch.

Then, I heard the sniff again and looked toward the door.

"Miss Fifi will see you now," the butler said. I followed him across the hall to the grand room. He opened the door and announced, "Mr. Ralph Miller" — as if her highness would not have recognized me if he had not told her.

The grand room was dimly lit but I had no trouble seeing Fifi. She sat on a high-backed blue satin chair looking like a white goddess. The spotlights in the ceiling were aimed directly at her fluffy fur making it glitter like snow in the moonlight.

Fifi - her grand grandness.

Always sensing the right moment and the proper gesture, Fifi waited until I walked the length of the room before she said a word. When at last I stood before her, she finally spoke in soft and precise tones.

"Ralph, darling," she said. "How kind of you to come."

"It was nice of you to invite me," I replied.

"Please sit down," she said gesturing to a short, but very comfortable chair, where I had no choice but to look from my lowness to her highness.

"Mr. Bruno tells me that you want to be a writer," she remarked.

"Yes," I answered.

"I think that's charming, darling, utterly charming," she said. "I'm impressed, Ralph, really impressed. You, entering the world of Keats and Shelly and Emerson and Shakespeare."

"Well, I don't know if my work would ever be compared with writers of such skill," I replied.

"Nonsense, you are too modest," she scolded. "Shame on you. I knew you were into languages, talking with people and such, but I had no idea that you were a literary genius as well. Mr. Bruno tells me you are writing a book."

"Tea is served, ma'am," the butler sniffed, as he carried a tray into the room.

"Thank you," Fifi said, dropping her eyelids.

The milk bone was delicious, but I can't say I cared much for the tea.

"I've recently returned from touring the East Coast," Fifi informed me. "Photographers snapping pictures and flashbulbs going off all the time."

"Must be tiring," I said.

"Dreadful, dear boy, absolutely dreadful," replied Fifi, waving her paw. "The personal appearances, the autograph seekers — no time to call my own. Fame is so demanding. It takes so much and gives back so little in return."

"I can imagine," I told her.

"But the show must go on," she said heroically. "The judges watching your every move. The cute young hopefuls wiggling their tails — constantly fluffing their fur and batting their eyelashes — anything for attention. But they are all show. They have no respect for style and grace."

"Hmmmm," I uttered, not knowing what else to say.

"Ralph," Fifi said suddenly. "I asked you here for a reason. I am ready to write my memoirs. It will be entitled, 'Poetry in Style and Grace', with the subtitle, 'The Story of a True Champion', written by the greatest champion of them all — Miss Fifi. And here's my surprise. It will also read, 'as told by Ralph Miller.'"

"I don't know what to say," I admitted.

"I realize what a surprise this must be, my dear," she continued. "My offering an unpublished writer such as yourself such a tremendous opportunity. Oh, Ralph, I can see it now — the story about a sweet and humble girl, but of course from the best of stock — who rises to fame and fortune yet who never loses her love and consideration for the common people. We will tell of the triumphs and the tragedies, the aspirations and the heartbreaks. The endless line of admirers hoping to touch the hem of my ribbon, begging for a lock of my fur, writing passionate notes on perfumed notecards. I plan to tell about them all."

"Oh, Ralph," she exclaimed. "It will go straight to the top of the best seller list — the *New York Times*, the cover of *Time Magazine*, *Newsweek*, *Life*, *People*, *US*. Isn't it exciting, Ralph? You can come over here every day and I will tell you one fascinating story after another. Of course, you must take it all down in longhand — no type-writers! I can't stand the sound of machinery."

"But I'm already working on a book," I inter-rupted.

"What's it about?" Fifi looked startled.

"It's about people's injustices to people. It's about the need for better understanding and toler-ance. It's about the hope for a better world."

"No one wants to read that boring stuff," Fifi sneered. "They want to read about movie stars and champions. They want personalities — Jane Fonda, Linda Ronstadt, and Olivia Newton-John. And they want to know more about Fifi. We'll have them standing in lines at the bookstores."

"Oh, I'm sure you will," I told her. "It sounds like a wonderful book, but it isn't one I want to write."

"I see," Fifi said in icy tones, stiffening her back.

She reached out, pressed a buzzer on the side of her chair. The doors opened and the butler stepped inside.

"Mr. Miller is leaving," she said coldly.

"Thank you for the tea and milk bone," I said standing up.

There was no answer.

41

"This way, please," the butler sniffed and I followed him from the room. I passed the marble statue which stood in the hallway. I had no sooner stepped outside when the door was slammed shut behind me.

As I started across the lawn, I saw Bruno waiting by the curb.

"And how is her majesty?" Bruno inquired.

"Majestic," I replied.

"As one might expect," he said. "I have news — Daschell is going to try to get out of the East Side this Friday night. If all goes right, he should be here sometime on Saturday."

"Terrific!" I exclaimed.

"Ralph," Bruno quietly warned. "I don't want you to build your hopes too high. The word I received isn't too optimistic. It seems the years and the wounds that Daschell has endured have taken their toll. They say he's not the detective he used to be."

"Well, we'll have to wait and see, won't we?" I said.

"Yes," Bruno replied, and we walked quietly toward home.

MAKE WAY, HEMINGWAY!

If Daschell had heard we needed him, and *if* he was willing to help, and *if* he could fight his way out of the East Side — *if, if, if* — how I hated that word! *If* elephants could fly, we would have to drive around in armored tanks.

Daschell would come on Saturday. We would have to wait four days. Four days — that seemed like a lifetime to me. Why does everything take so long?

I had a choice to make. I could either sit around and mope or I could go back to the typewriter and destroy the power of the white. I knew what I had to do. Moping around wouldn't help pass the time and it certainly wouldn't find Josie, wherever she was.

I soon learned that a writer doesn't wait for inspiration or for ideas. If you are serious about writing — you write. It is while you are writing that the inspiration comes and the ideas start popping like firecrackers. As Mr. Melton has written in one of his books, "The best ideas come from the work and not from our heads." I didn't understand that at first, but now I do. Once I sit down and begin writing, the act of writing starts giving me ideas. I am soon transformed to another plane of existence and I become an open receiver of thoughts. It's really spooky and wonderful. It is like having the Bluebird of Happiness, the Wizard of Oz, and E.T. all rolled into one. I highly recommend it.

And then on Friday morning, it happened. I wrote:

>And so it is, in this world of conflicts, we must rise above the prejudices of the past — we should stop judging others by the color of their skin and by their appearances. We must realize that we are created from the same fabric of life. It is in our sameness that we are allowed to understand the sorrows and share the joys of others. And we are also different and

        unique. It is the uniqueness of each individual
        that offers a vast variety of ideas and approaches
        to life and makes life such an exciting adventure.
        Yes, we are all the same — only different.

It was done. It was the last paragraph of the last page of the last chapter of my first book. I wanted to run outside and stand in the street and cheer loud enough for everyone to hear. "I did it, I've written a book!" Of course, I didn't do such a thing. One must maintain some control over such urges.

However, before Jeff and Tim left for school, I showed them the manuscript. Tim said the typing looked neat and hoped I might help him with his term paper. Jeff wanted to know if it would make a good movie. Neither offered to read it — brothers can really be inconsiderate clods.

But Mother read it, stopping only long enough to brush tears from her eyes. Of course, she loved it. What else would you expect from a mother?

And that night, Dad sat and read my manuscript. There were no tears from Dad but he did chuckle several times revealing that my sense of humor had not gone unnoticed. I liked that.

When he finished, he closed the cover and said thoughtfully, "It's good, Ralph."

Although I would have been happier with a "terrific" or a "wow," I knew that a "good" from Dad was equal to a "wow" from anyone else.

"Now, what are you going to do with it?" he wanted to know.

"I'm going to send it to a publisher," I told him.

He was quiet for a moment and then said, "Ralph, I hope you realize that publishers receive thousands of manuscripts and most of them never get published. Don't build your hopes too high. No matter how good your book may be, the editor may reject it."

"If the editor rejects it," I told him, "I won't be disappointed — I'll be grateful. If the editor turns down this book, it will only mean that I've sent it to a dumb editor. And I don't want some dummy publishing my book."

"Well," he replied, "are you going to send it to a small, local publisher?"

"I've thought about that," I told him. "I figure that maybe a small publisher wouldn't have as much money to gamble on the work of an unknown writer as a big one. So, I've decided to send it to the biggest and the richest publisher in the country. *Writer's Market* says the biggest publisher is Apex. So, I'm sending my manuscript to the Apex Publishing Company in New York."

"But what if they don't even read it?" he asked.

"Oh, they will," I told him. "I wrote a letter to the editor two weeks ago and yesterday, I got a reply. It said she was eager to see my book."

"Okay, Hemingway," my father laughed, shaking his head in disbelief. "It's your book — send it."

I have never understood why adults spend so much time preparing children for failure and rejection. After all, how much do we need to learn about failure? Not much. All of us can fail without any preparation at all. Instead, adults should spend more time teaching us how to succeed. As I always say, "Nothing ventured, nothing gained."

On Saturday morning, I placed my manuscript in a box and wrapped it in brown paper. Dad took me to the post office and we mailed my hopes and my dreams to an editor I had never met. But I wasn't worried about it. For now, I would have to turn my attention to more pressing matters — Josie. I had to find Josie.

"Have you heard from Daschell?" I asked Bruno.

"I heard there was a big rumble in the East Side last night," he replied. "Several were injured. Rumor has it that Daschell was involved. But no one knows for sure."

I quickly subtracted one from two and came up with one. I figured that it was probably either the bulldog or the chihuahua who passed the rumors to Bruno. Although I wondered who they were, I didn't ask.

As for Daschell, all we could do was wait and hope for the best. I began to suspect that Saturday would be a long day.

7

THE OLD WARRIOR

Saturday proved to be longer than I thought. After it was dark outside, I went over to Bruno's house and we kept our vigil together. Well, almost — Bruno slept most of the time, snoring away the lonely hours. Nine o'clock — ten o'clock — eleven-thirty — and still no sign of Daschell.

Then, when it was almost midnight, Bruno suddenly stirred from a sound sleep and slowly raised his head. I couldn't hear anything but Bruno had sensed something I had missed.

"Hi yuh, Bruno." We heard a voice from the darkness.

"We thought you were lost," Bruno remarked.

"A bad penny always turns up," the voice replied.

"Did you have much trouble getting out?" Bruno asked.

"Like the Fourth of July."

"So I heard," Bruno replied.

"They got the runt about a week ago," Daschell said.

"How?" Bruno asked.

"They caught him off guard," he replied. "They never would have gotten him in the old days — not the runt. He was fast as greased lightning. But the years slowed him down."

"Who did it?" Bruno wondered.

"A gang of worthless punks. But it wasn't as easy as they thought. The runt took three of 'em down with him."

"What about the others?" Bruno inquired.

"I took care of all five of them last night," Daschell replied. "They won't bother anyone else."

"Are you all right?" Bruno asked, standing up.

Daschell - the night visitor.

"I think I got a couple of cracked ribs," Daschell remarked.

"Are you in pain?" Bruno asked.

"Only when I breathe," Daschell said.

Bruno tore a long piece of material from his bedding. "Come on, Ralph," he said, "I'll need your help."

I followed Bruno to the corner of the yard. As the clouds floated away from the moon, I could see a gray shepherd standing by the back fence — bent but not broken — his fur jagged and torn. He was pale and thin — his bones poked through his skin. His steel gray eyes had seen more than most. The pouches under his eyes were heavy and swollen and there was a jagged scar across his face. It wasn't a new scar — it had healed years before. But as Bruno wrapped the strips of material tightly around Daschell's chest, I could see other scars — some of them older than the one on his face. There were fresh cuts too, undoubtedly trophies of more recent battles.

"You old warrior," Bruno told him. "You really look a mess."

"So what's new?" Daschell retorted.

"How long since your last meal?" Bruno asked.

"Two, maybe three days. I lost count."

Bruno placed his bowl before his friend, but the shepherd took only three or four bites. Then he stopped and looked straight at me.

"Are you the talker?" he asked.

"Yes."

"We had a talker on the squad years ago," Daschell said. "Good undercover cop. Better than a tape recorder. People would say anything in front of him — never guessing he could repeat what he heard."

"Wasn't that Frankie?" Bruno asked.

"Yeh. Funny little guy," Daschell mused. "Looked like a mutt but he had the heart of a thoroughbred."

"What happened to him?" I inquired.

"They gave him his walking papers," Daschell said with disgust. "They got them little fingernail-sized microphones now. It's not like it used to be, Bruno. The young ones have taken over. Everything's computers today. Put a name in the slot and the numbers come out. They got no need for furry mutts or us old detectives. Mickey the Kid, Granny the Grub, and the Runt — they're all gone now."

"I know," said Bruno.

"Okay, kid," Daschell said, looking at me. "Tell me about it — and I mean everything — from start to finish."

So I did. I told him about the mysterious black sedan and about being kidnapped by the fat one and the skinny one. I told him about the Boss and how Josie and I escaped from the farmhouse. And about how they came back and took her away from the police station.

After I had finished, Bruno looked at Daschell.

"Ever hear of these guys before?" he asked.

"Could be," Daschell replied. "Think the fat one used to be known as 'Little Eddie.'"

"Little?" I exclaimed. "Why he's as big as a hippopotamus!"

"Yeh, but his brother was bigger," Daschell said. "And they called the brother 'Big Eddie' so this one was tagged 'Little Eddie.' A cheap hood. Not too bright in the head department. Originally from St. Louie — in and out of the slammer more times than you could count. Mostly petty stuff — grabbing old women's purses and sticking up gas stations."

"What about the skinny one?" I asked.

"I think I know who he is," Daschell replied.

54

"Originally from New York, he has several aliases — 'The Bronx Dude,' 'The Central Park Crud,' 'The Hackensack Creep.' Then, he started wearing cowboy boots and twirling this little rope. They tagged him 'The Cowboy.'"

"That's him," I said.

"Yeh," Daschell replied. "Thought so. Believe it or not, he's dumber than Big Eddie and Little Eddie put together."

"And what about the Boss?" I wanted to know.

"Don't ring no bell," Daschell said. "Except . . . there's something . . . just can't place it."

He looked back to me and said, "It would help most if you could remember the way back to the farmhouse. We might find a clue there."

"I've tried," I told him. "It's all too hazy. We were running most of the time and it was night."

"Well," he said. "Try to put it together. We need everything we can get."

"All right," I promised.

"I better take off now," Daschell said suddenly, looking around.

"Why don't you stay the night here?" Bruno offered.

"Better not," Daschell replied. "I may have been

followed. Didn't see no one but you never know."

"How can we contact you?" I wanted to know.

"You don't," he said. "I know where to find you. I'll be back in a few days."

And, suddenly, he was gone. It was as if the shadows of the night had swallowed him before our eyes.

"Well, we better get some sleep," Bruno yawned.

"Why wouldn't he tell us where he would be?" I asked.

"He's on the run," Bruno replied.

"Who is after him?" I asked.

"New enemies and old ghosts from the past," Bruno replied.

"Do you think they will find him?" I wondered.

"He may get away from his enemies," Bruno said thoughtfully, "but the ghosts of the past will always run with him."

"What do you mean?" I started to ask, but was stopped by the sound of snoring from Bruno's house. Although I had many questions, I realized there would be no more answers tonight.

I went home.

THE TRICKY LITTLE WALNUT

Morning came in gray haze. I hadn't slept well. I had spent most of the night probing my mind — trying, without much success, to recall the paths Josie and I had traveled in our escape from the Boss's farmhouse. I could remember seeing bushes and trees and the headlights of the mysterious black sedan. I could remember crossing highways and racing down dirt roads; but it was nothing more than the quick and fleeting images one sees in a nightmare.

The Psychologist —
more hocus and pocus.

Dad offered to help. In the afternoon, he and I got into the car and we drove for hours and hours. We saw a lot of fields and traveled one side road after another. We must have looked at more than a thousand farmhouses. If any of them was the place we were searching for, I didn't recognize it. Finally, we returned to our home.

"Any luck?" Tim asked, as we entered the house.

"No," I admitted. "I think my brains are all scrambled."

"Maybe you should see a shrink," Jeff quipped.

"Jeff!" I exclaimed. "You're the smartest brother in the whole world!"

"What'd I say?" he wondered.

"See a shrink. That's exactly what I need to do," I said, jumping up on the couch and throwing a pillow into the air.

"Well, if you act like that," said Tim, "you certainly should."

"I thought you would be back," the psychologist said as Dad and I entered his office.

"I'm pleased to see you, too," I said. "What made you think I would be back?"

"All those psychoses and neuroses floating around in your fuzzy little head," the psychologist replied. "The endless questions. Who am I? What am I? Where am I going?"

"I know who I am," I told him. "I'm Ralph Miller. And I know what I am. I'm a boy who happens to look like a dog. And I also know where I'm going — straight to the top of the best seller list. What I really need to learn is where I've been."

"Ahhh. It's worse than I thought," he exclaimed, wiggling his eyebrows up and down, making his face look as if it was about to fly.

"Let me explain," my father said.

He told the psychologist the whole story — or at least as much as he needed to know.

When my father finished, the psychologist said, "That's all very interesting. What do you want from me?"

"I want you to hypnotize me," I told him. "I must find the farmhouse."

"I don't know about this," he said. "The brain is a very tricky little walnut."

"Haven't you ever hypnotized anyone before?" I asked.

"Oh, many times," he replied, "but . . ."

"But never a dog," I interrupted.

"Ralph," my father scolded.

"I don't mean to be rude," I said, "but isn't that why you are hesitating?"

"It did cross my mind," he admitted. "You see, when you were here before, I didn't mind helping you get into school. Yours was a very interesting case. I saw it more as a study — Ralph Miller versus the structures of society. As you know, the principal was very opposed to the idea of your entering school. He threw a curve ball and sent you to me and I bounced you right back at him to see how he would respond. It nearly drove him bananas."

"I see," I said. "So I was nothing more than a Ping-Pong ball bounced back and forth by the two of you.'

"No, no, it was all very scientific — nothing personal, you understand," he insisted.

"Yes, I think I do," I said. "Kick the boy and see who barks."

"It seemed like a good idea at the time," he said.

"Well," I said, taking a deep breath. "Then was then and now is now. I've got to find that farmhouse and Josie's life hangs in the balance. Are you going to help me or not?"

The psychologist finally nodded his head in agreement. "I don't promise anything — but I will try."

He took his watch from his pocket and told me to lean back in my chair.

"Relax," he said, as his watch began to swing back and forth like a pendulum. "Just relax. Count backward from ten to zero. When you reach zero, you will be in a deep hypnotic trance. You will answer all of my questions truthfully. Begin counting."

I began, "Ten, nine, eight, seven, six. . . ." And in my mind, I floated down, down, down a spiral staircase, descending from reality into my subconscious. "Five, four, three, two, one, zero." My mind drifted into a new awareness — and at last, I was there and not there.

"Ralph," the psychologist said. "I want you to return to that final day at school. Do you see the classroom?"

"Yes," I answered.

"And what is the weather like outside?" he asked.

"Cloudy, looks like it's going to rain."

"And does it start to rain?"

"Yes, when Jeff and Tim and I are walking home. We see the lightning and we hear thunder. Suddenly, it starts raining. 'Hurry, Jeff! Come on, Tim.'"

"And what happens?"

"I don't know. What's going on? Something's over my face. It's a net. Someone grabs me up and pushes me into a box. It's dark and I can't see. Hmmmmmmmmmmmmmmmmmmmmmmmmmm."

"What's that noise?" the psychologist wanted to know.

"It's the mysterious black sedan. All the cylinders are finely ground and ready to go."

"What happens?"

"It goes. I'm in the trunk and it's a rough ride."

"Ralph," the psychologist said. "Now the car has stopped at the farmhouse. Can you see the house?"

"No, I'm still inside the box. I smell cigar smoke. The fat one is smoking a cigar. It stinks. Now, the box is carried into the farmhouse. We stop. Someone is unlocking the box. It opens. I try to run but I'm caught. The fat one grabs me. Yuck!"

"What happens?"

"I bite his hand — it tastes awful — like cigars

and onions. He starts to hit me."

"What do you do?"

"I play dog and start barking. 'You've got the wrong dog,' someone yells. 'You idiots!'"

"Who says that?"

"The Boss."

"What does he look like?" the psychologist asked.

"Pudgy, like a marshmallow," I answered. "Then, the fat one and the skinny one begin arguing. I try to get away."

"And do you escape?"

"I am running down a hallway. I hear a voice from the other side of a door. It's a girl, she's locked in the room. Held captive. 'I'll help you.'"

"What do you do now?" the psychologist asked.

"I go back and start talking — smart like. The Boss is delighted because he now has another talking dog. Then, he orders the fat one and the skinny one to grab me. They throw me in a room and lock the door."

"What do you see in the room?"

"It's dark. There's a window, but it's night. I can't see — but I think someone else is in the room. There is! It's the girl — Josie."

"Now, what do you do?" the psychologist asked.

"We plan to escape. I push the dresser to the window. Crash! I smash the window. Oh, oh, they hear it. They're coming! 'Jump, Josie, Jump!' She'll never make it! The door opens. The fat one is in the room — but he's too late. We jump out the window and run across the field."

"What does the house look like"

"Don't know, I can't see. It's behind us."

"All right," the psychologist said. "Stop where you are and turn around."

"Okay."

"Are you in front of the house?"

"Yes."

"Look at it. What does it look like?"

"It's old," I reply. "Looks deserted. Some of the windows are boarded up."

"What else do you see?"

"To the right, there's an old barn, half fallen down. And to the left, there's a windmill — but I don't think it works — two of the blades are bent."

"Is there a street number on the house or a mailbox?"

"No. There's an old post but the mailbox is gone."

"All right, Ralph. Now turn and run to the nearest road," the psychologist suggested.

"I'm running but not far — maybe a half mile — there is a road."

"Good. Do you see a road sign?"

"Yes," I reply. "It says Old *something*. Old *something* Road. Now I see it — it says Old *Mill* Road."

"Good boy!" the psychologist declared and then stopped for a moment. "Now, Ralph, I have only one more question and you must answer it truthfully."

"Okay," I consented.

"As soon as you answer the question, you may wake up and remember everything you have seen," the psychologist told me. "The question is — are you a dog or are you a boy?"

"I am a boy," I said immediately and woke up.

"Pretty sneaky, Doc," I remarked.

"Sorry," he said, "but I had to know. Still I think it would be a good idea for you to come in for treatment."

"Don't think so," I said. "My id may be odd but it's the only one I've got and I think I'll keep it the way it is. I know what I came to learn. The farmhouse is on Old Mill Road and I remember what it looks like. Thank you."

"And what about you, Mr. Miller?" the psychologist said to my father. "You and your wife must be under tremendous stress — having such a son."

My father smiled and replied, "If you think he's bad, you should see the other two we have at home."

"I wouldn't dare," gasped the psychologist, peering over his glasses.

Dad and I laughed all the way home.

THE BUBBLE GUM BANDIT

Three days passed and we heard nothing from Daschell.

On Monday, a letter came from the editor of Apex Publishing Company. I tore it open. It read, in part:

Dear Mr. Miller,

We love your book. Enclosed is a contract and a copy. Please sign both. (One is for your files and please return the other for ours.) As you will see, we are offering you an advance of $6,000 against royalties. $3,000 will be paid to you once you have signed the contracts and the remaining $3,000 upon publication of your book. We hope these terms are agreeable.

Agreeable? If the editor had been standing there,

I would have licked her face. For the lack of a better word — WOW!

And then, I read the last paragraph:

Due to the importance of your book, we are working the typesetters overtime and plan to ship to bookstores within the next two weeks. We have contacted the Tonight Show and are arranging a guest spot for you to coincide with the publication date.

Yours truly,

Carla Marla

The Editor

Oh, oh — a guest appearance on the Tonight Show. Now, I had still another problem to consider — national television, coast to coast. Fame! I hadn't planned on that.

When I showed the letter to my family, Mom said she wasn't surprised at all. But, of course, Dad was astounded. The attitudes of Jeff and Tim changed 180 degrees.

"I want to read that book now," Jeff said eagerly. "I think I might write one this summer."

And Tim suggested that perhaps I should have an agent to handle all the business arrangements. Obviously, he was applying for the job.

I knew it was not the merits of my literary work that had captured the interest of my brothers — it was the money!

After reviewing my thoughts and doubts, I signed the contracts. I would have to find some way to deal with the television stuff — later — but not much later because I only had two weeks to think of something. But what? I wondered.

Later that morning when I heard Bruno barking, I knew he wanted to see me and I immediately ran over.

"I told Daschell about the Old Mill Road," Bruno said. "He will meet us at the farmhouse at nine o'clock tonight."

"Are you sure he can find it?" I asked.

"Ralph," Bruno grumbled. "Daschell is one of the ten best detectives in the world. If he can't find the farmhouse on Old Mill Road, then how do you think he will ever find the Boss and Josie?"

"Right," I said, realizing that sometimes I really had a dumb mouth.

Knowing that the trip to the farmhouse would be a long walk for Bruno, I suggested that Dad take us in the car. But Bruno wouldn't hear of it. He said if

The farmhouse —
a nightmare revisited.

we brought a stranger with us we would never see Daschell again. So, I agreed. We would walk.

To allow enough time, Bruno and I left our homes a little after sundown. Although I could tell Bruno's arthritic shoulder was causing him considerable discomfort, my friend never uttered a word of complaint. The cold wind moaned through the bushes and the light of the moon cast eerie shadows across the empty fields. When at last we saw the farmhouse, it was exactly as I had seen it under hypnosis — the windows boarded up, the old barn to the right, the broken windmill with two bent blades to the left.

Discovering that the front door was locked, Bruno and I made our way around to the back of the house. I saw the broken window from which Josie and I had made our narrow escape. When Bruno touched the back door, it creaked and opened wide. Cautiously, we entered the house and walked down the hallway. I saw the room where Josie and I had been held captive. When Bruno and I entered the big room, even in the darkness of the night, I could see that all the paintings and the pieces of sculpture had been removed.

"They took everything of value," we heard a

voice say.

"I say, Daschell," Bruno scolded. "You gave us a start."

"You mean they didn't leave a clue?" I asked.

"Didn't say that," Daschell remarked, holding out a small piece of paper.

"Why it's a bubble gum wrapper," I responded.

"Right," Daschell replied. "They're all over the place."

"But what do they mean?" I wondered.

"They mean," Daschell told us, "that we aren't dealing with an ordinary hoodlum. We are up against a genius — a mastermind of the first order."

"The Boss?" I asked.

"The Boss," he confirmed. "Except he wasn't known as the Boss when I first heard of him. He was called the 'Bubble Gum Bandit.'"

"The Bubble Gum Bandit?" I exclaimed.

"You may recall the incident, Bruno," Daschell said. "About six years ago, *someone* realized that bubble gum was big business. Kids all across the country were addicted to it. Some couldn't watch a movie or read a book without a wad of the rubbery stuff stuck between their teeth. A filthy habit. Some kids had it so bad they couldn't eat breakfast without first having a chew. Pressing their tongues against the stuff and blowing it up like balloons, they looked like their insides were coming out of their mouths."

"Disgusting," Bruno remarked.

"Anyway," Daschell continued. "This *someone* started buying up all the bubble gum factories on the sly — under different names — so no one would guess what he was doing. After he bought all the factories, he stopped all shipments of the stuff. Within days all the stores ran out of bubble gum."

"I remember that," Bruno said.

"You should, it made front page headlines," Daschell replied. "It was called the 'Great Bubble Gum Panic of '77.' Kids were desperate. For awhile, they bought the stuff at black market prices, but even that source dried up. The president had to send in the army to stand guard at all the movie theaters and restaurants to keep kids from peeling off used globs that were stuck under seats and tables."

"How disgusting," I remarked.

"Chewing bubble gum's a tough habit to break," Daschell said. "They had to give tranquilizers to some of the kids. Many of them had the shakes so bad they had to go to bed. Schools were closed."

"So what happened?" I wanted to know.

"About two weeks later, shipments started arriving at the stores — but not at five cents a package. Now, the price skyrocketed to a buck a wad. It made no difference to the kids — they would pay any amount. They formed lines in front of the candy stores and supermarkets. And the Bubble Gum Bandit made millions and millions of dollars."

"Didn't they ever catch him?" I asked.

"We tried, but by the time the police discovered what had happened, the bandit had taken the money and run."

"But didn't this Bubble Gum Bandit ever come out of hiding?"

"Never," Daschell said. "But we did start hearing about some guy who was buying up famous paintings, statues, and things like that — you know, rare items."

"Like talking dogs?" I interjected.

"Could be," Daschell nodded. "Anyway, although we had no proof, some of us began to suspect that this guy — who we called 'the Collector' and the 'Bubble Gum Bandit' — might be one and the same. Made sense because who else had that kind of money to throw around? And now, he has surfaced again — but this time as 'the Boss.'"

"What can we do?" Bruno wondered.

"We've got to find some way to get him out in the open," Daschell replied. "What we need is a pigeon — a decoy — we've got to show the Boss something so unique and so beautiful he'd have to own it or else."

"Like another talking dog?" I asked.

"Not just *another* talking dog," Daschell replied thoughtfully. "He already has Josie. We've got to show him the most beautiful, the most elegant talking dog in the world. A talking dog that will make his eyes pop right out of his head."

I looked at Bruno. I could see an idea beginning to form . . . an idea not to my liking.

"No, Bruno," I said. "It won't work. She can't talk and she wouldn't do it if she could. She isn't even speaking to me. She won't do it."

"*She*," said Bruno, "would run through a burning forest carrying a can of gasoline for attention."

"No," I said. "No, no, no — not Fifi!"

THE SETUP

Daschell and Bruno laid out the most idiotic scheme I ever heard. It was crazy, really crazy. Although I argued that Fifi would not take part in such an outrageous plan, Bruno insisted that she would. How did I get myself into such a mess, I wondered, not really wanting to hear the answer.

Shortly after lunch, Bruno and I were in front of Fifi's house. We followed the butler into the grand room to speak with her royal uppityness.

As we entered the grand room, Fifi nodded her head slightly, but didn't say, "Good afternoon," "Hi ya, boys," or "Kiss my foot." She just sat there in her high-backed chair with the spotlights aimed at her glistening fur.

"How kind of you to see us on such short notice," Bruno said politely.

"Please be seated," Fifi finally replied to Bruno. She didn't even look at me.

"We have a slight problem," Bruno said. "Ralph's publisher has arranged for him to make an appearance on the Tonight Show a week from Friday."

"I am aware that your friend has been dabbling in the arts," Fifi remarked, "but I had no idea that he was to be published so soon. What has that to do with me?"

"Oh, nothing," Bruno replied. "You see, Ralph is such a shy creature — the mere idea of appearing in public is very upsetting to him. If he refuses to be on the show, the publisher might cancel his contract. But if he does appear on the show, he might . . . well."

"I could throw up," I said bluntly.

"How graphic," Fifi exclaimed.

"Yes," Bruno agreed. "It is indeed a problem."

"What do you want me to do about it?" Fifi asked. "Coach him?"

"Oh, no," Bruno said, shaking his head. "I think it is quite hopeless. Ralph would never be able to make the appearance himself. So, we have a plan. Moments before Ralph is introduced, he will become suddenly ill and we'll need someone to take his place."

"And you want me to. . . ." Fifi started to say.

"Oh, no," Bruno interrupted. Knowing your busy schedule, we wouldn't dare ask you. What we wondered is, do you know of a lesser-known showgirl who might consider taking his place? Since the Tonight Show people expect a talking dog, we have this tiny mechanical device that can be hidden in her fur. Ralph will be doing the talking but it will appear as if she is answering the questions and saying all of the witty things that Ralph will utter."

Bruno certainly had Fifi's attention now. Thoughts of spotlights and cameras began racing through her head.

"It could prove to be an excellent opportunity for a young hopeful. It could make her a star," Bruno said. And once he had said it, he waited, his big brown eyes looking innocent of scheme or sham.

"There is no such girl," Fifi said, "who has the depth of emotion and the skill as an actress to make such a plan work. The person you seek must have the ability to mesmerize Mr. Carson and the entire audience. She must be an actress who possesses style and grace."

"Quite so," Bruno agreed.

"There is only one person in the whole world who could do such a thing," Fifi declared.

"Who?" Bruno asked.

"No one but yours truly," Fifi insisted.

"But *would* you?" Bruno wanted to know.

"I will wear a pink ribbon — no blue — the color of sincerity, and Mr. Paul must do my hair. And as for you, Buster," Fifi suddenly growled, looking straight at me. "Everything I say better be funny or you won't live to tell the tale."

"Yes, ma'am," I found myself agreeing.

Oh, Ralph, what have you done? I wondered.

11

"THE SHOW MUST GO ON!"

The airplane arrived in Los Angeles shortly after noon. In less than three hours, we had flown from winter to summer. Everywhere we looked there were suntanned people wearing brightly colored clothes and dark glasses.

My editor had said a woman from the publicity department would meet us at the terminal. I thought she might take one look at me and my companions and run for her life. But when she saw

The Publicist —
Hooray for Hollywood!

Daschell, Bruno, Fifi, and me in the doorway, she didn't seem upset or even surprised. However, we later learned she had just handled the publicity for Mick Jagger's group only the week before. I guess our group must have seemed tame compared to the wild-haired antics of the Rolling Stones.

The publicist said we were to tape the Tonight Show at two o'clock in the afternoon and it would be aired that night.

"Every minute you are on the show, you must remember to sell the book," the publicist told me. "Mr. Carson may only hold up the book once and then talk about everything else but the book. He's an absolutely charming man — but your job is to keep bringing the conversation back to your book."

"I'll try," I promised.

As we entered the NBC studios, I could tell the publicist was well-versed in all the "show biz" talk — she called everyone "sweetie," "sugar," and "honeycakes," and kissed them like they were long lost cousins. Then, she led us to a small room where we were to wait.

"Mr. Carson never talks with his guest before the show," she told us. "He wants the conversation on the show to be fresh and new."

"Oh, it will be," I nodded, looking at my three friends who were sitting on the other side of the room.

My companions were as cool as cucumbers. Daschell sat stone-faced and Bruno appeared to be half-asleep. Fifi, to my surprise, had not yipped one yip since we arrived in town. No one could ever have guessed that it would be she, instead of me, who would be a guest on the Tonight Show. "What an old pro," I said to myself. But I wasn't calm — I was a bundle of nerves. It won't work! It won't work! *It won't work* kept running through my head.

Finally, Daschell slyly nodded toward the TV set which stood in the corner of the room. I understood.

"Will my friends be able to watch the show on that television?" I asked the publicist.

"Sure they can, honeycakes," she said. "Or I can arrange for them to sit in the audience, if you prefer."

"Oh, no. They are very shy around people," I replied. "I'm sure they would rather watch it in here.

"I understand, sweetie," she replied.

"Sweetie" or not, she didn't understand — she just

thought she did. But the rest understood my question and the importance of her answer. Now we knew I could stay in this room, see the show, hear Mr. Carson's questions and even watch Fifi's mouth move while I did the talking. It was a perfect setup. All I had to do was get ready to be sick — considering my state of nervousness, that was going to be easy

A man came into the room carrying a clipboard and told us the show would begin in five minutes. He said there would be two other guests who would be on the show before me and that he would come and get me when it was time. Then, the man turned on the television set and left the room. The final countdown had begun.

The show started and Ed McMahon said, "And hereee's Johnny!" As promised, there he was — standing in the spotlight.

"Did you ever see the smog as thick as it was today?" Mr. Carson asked the audience.

"How smoggy was it?" the audience chorused.

"Well," he quipped. "The smog was so thick that the sea gulls had to use radar to find the beach."

The audience laughed and Mr. Carson was off and running — telling one joke after another. The interview with the first guest — a young comedian who stuttered — went well. Then, an actor on a daytime soap opera told of his long list of accomplishments (which turned out to be no more than his being on a daytime soap opera).

As far as the Tonight Show goes, it wasn't the best of shows and it wasn't the worst of shows, but I realized that it was nearly three-quarters finished and our turn was next. Daschell checked the miniature speaker skillfully hidden in Fifi's furry locks. It was OK.

When the man opened the door and said, "Mr. Miller," I stood up, grabbed at my chest, let out a loud howl and pretended to pass out on the floor.

The next thirty seconds were mass confusion.

"What's the matter," someone said.

"Get him on his feet," panicked another voice.

"What will we do?"

There must have been ten people crowded in the room by now. Someone's voice finally said, "Isn't that Miss Fifi, the international poodle champion?"

"Where?"

"There."

"Yes, it is."

"Put her on in his place."

"Great!"

And they whisked her out of the room.

No one had seemed to notice or care that it was I who had said many of those things—and it had worked. When I said I wanted to be alone, Bruno acted quickly. He pushed the publicist out the door and he and Daschell stood guard. I jumped up and looked at the television set.

"Our next guest is an unusual person," Mr. Carson was saying, holding up my book. "He is the author of a new book, **We Are All Alike — Only Different.** Mr. Ralph M . . . "

When he was handed a note, he stopped.

"I just received a note," he said, "which says that Mr. Miller has been suddenly taken ill backstage. But, we are fortunate to have in his place, Miss Fifi, the international champion of poodles, who, I am told, can talk. She can *what?* It says here she *can talk.* That's what it says, folks. Will you please welcome Miss Fifi."

The camera moved to the curtain of many colors, the spotlight came on and there she was — Miss Fifi herself — her snow-white fur sparkling in the lime-light. She held a pose for a moment and then didn't walk but literally glided across the stage and took her seat.

The audience applauded.

"Is it true that you can talk?" Mr. Carson inquired.

It was my turn, but I waited for Fifi to move her lips. Actress that she was, she lowered her eyelids and slyly smiled.

"Can buzzards fly?" my voice and her lips answered in perfect unison.

"You really can talk," Mr. Carson declared.

"And so can you, darling," we responded. "Isn't it thrilling?"

"And how long have you been talking?" he asked.

"Since I was a pup in pantaloons," she remarked. "I remember my dear mother — of course a grand champion herself — had taken me to Paris — France, you know. At dinner one night at Chez Jolie, I didn't like the meal that had been ordered for me. So, I told the waiter what I wanted — in French, of course."

"In French?" Mr. Carson exclaimed.

"Of course, darling," she replied. "As I always say, when in Rome, one must do as the Romans do."

"And you speak Italian, too?"

"Uno poco," we replied.

"How many languages do you speak?" he wondered.

"Eight, no nine, if you count English," Fifi mimed. "And why not? It sure beats howling at the moon."

"And I bet you've done plenty of that in your time."

"I still do," she laughed. "Oh, Johnny, you dirty dog."

The audience howled. They loved her. Fifi was a hit. And she kept getting better. She fluttered her eyelashes and wiggled her nose. She cooed. She flirted. Her timing was perfect. She was wonderful. And if I do say so myself, my retorts were quick and right on target. I couldn't believe it — it was nothing but fun. I was having the time of my life.

"I do hope Mr. Miller is all right," I suddenly said and Fifi had no choice but to move her lips and follow along. "Have you read his book?" she asked.

"Well," Mr. Carson admitted, "not all of it."

"You must," she insisted. And then she turned to the audience, "All of you must read it, too. It's a

Fifi and Mr. Carson —

my words and her mouth

marvelous book — a work of genius."

"Hold up the book again, darling," she urged.

And Mr. Carson did as he was commanded.

"Remember the title, **We Are All Alike — Only Different.** Now, I want all of you to do something for Fifi," we said with quiet sincerity. "First thing tomorrow morning, run to your nearest bookstore and buy a copy. You will love it," Fifi insisted. "Now promise."

"We promise!" The audience cheered.

Even Mr. Carson said he would not sleep that night until he had finished my book.

And then, I quickly wrapped everything up in a neat package for the benefit of the Boss. I mentioned that Fifi lived in Prairie Village and even told the name of the street. If the Boss watched the show that night he would simply *have* to add Fifi to his collection. And if he didn't see the show, he would certainly hear about it because there was no doubt that, in less than fifteen minutes, a star was born. Miss Fifi had arrived. She came. She saw. She conquered!

After the show we were all so excited we could hardly contain ourselves. The publicist said it was the best send-off a book ever had. The publisher was happy; Daschell was pleased; it made Bruno sleepy and, of course, Fifi was riding on a cloud.

We had done it!

However, it wasn't until we were on the airplane — heading toward home — that I suddenly realized what we had really done. We had shown the Boss this marvelous talking dog. We had told him where she lived. We had just placed Fifi's life in the gravest peril!

12

THE DECOY'S DECOY

"Do you realize what we've done?" I said to Bruno. "We have thoughtlessly placed Fifi's life in danger."

"We'll protect her. We're her friends," Bruno replied.

"With friends like us, Fifi doesn't need any enemies," I snapped.

"You didn't go into this blindfolded," Bruno pointed out.

"I should have had my head examined," I fumed. "That's what I get for becoming involved with an ex-beauty queen, a washed-up detective on the run, and a worn-out old codger who would rather sleep."

"I don't recall," Bruno replied, "that you were so particular when you asked for our help."

Of course, he was right.

"I'm sorry, Bruno," I told him. "Please forgive me."

"Consider it done," Bruno said. "I think you are overreacting, Ralph. Daschell should return any moment and, from this time forward, the three of us will stand guard at Fifi's house. Let the fat one or the skinny one or the Boss try anything and we will nab them on the spot."

"But what if we don't?" I worried. "What if they outsmart us and make off with Fifi?"

"Well, if you want to know the truth," Bruno chuckled, "I doubt they would survive one day. I hardly think that the Boss, the fat one and the skinny one, Genghis Khan and the Russian Army — all together — would be a match for the Lady Fifi. She would drive them to the edge of insanity in less than an hour. In fact, I shouldn't be surprised if they would offer us a handsome price to take her back."

"That's not funny," I snapped. "She musn't be kidnapped."

"There's where you're wrong." I heard Daschell's voice and I turned around.

"What do you mean?" I questioned, not believing my ears.

"They must take her," Daschell replied. "I thought you knew that. How else are we going to find their hideout?"

"We'll tie them up and make them talk," I proposed.

"You must be joking," Daschell scowled. "We're not dealing with sidewalk punks. We're taking on two hardened criminals and a mastermind. They'd never talk."

"We've got to call the whole thing off," I insisted. "I won't allow Fifi to be placed in such danger."

"I've been thinking about that, too," Daschell said. "Didn't set right with me either. So, I've come up with another plan."

"I don't want to hear it," I declared.

"I do," Bruno said, opening his eyes.

"You stay out of this," I scolded. "No more plans."

"Let me say one word," Daschell requested.

"Go right ahead," I said defiantly. "No one word will change my mind."

Daschell looked straight into my eyes and said one word — "Josie."

Drat!

"Okay, you've got me," I admitted. "I have the feeling I am going to regret it, but tell us the plan."

"The plan is," Daschell said, stepping closer, "not to let them kidnap Fifi, but someone who is made up to look like Fifi."

"Who could we get to do that?" I wondered.

"I didn't like the way Daschell and Bruno were looking at me.

"Oh, no," I exclaimed. "Not on your lives. I won't do it."

Everything will be all right I kept telling myself. Famous last words!

Like Marie Antoinette standing before the guillotine, saying, "I'm not going to lose my head over this."

Guess who!

Or Joan of Arc, tied to the stake, asking, "Does anyone have a match?"

Or General Custer leading his men into the Little Big Horn, saying, "Doesn't look like we'll see any Indians today."

The activities at Fifi's house reminded me of a chapter in my book which stresses that people and things are not always what they may appear to be. From the outside, everything on the inside looked absolutely normal. The butler served dinner to Miss Fifi in the dining room. And later, Miss Fifi sat in the grand room in her high-backed chair watching television. And finally, the television was turned off and it appeared as if the grand lady ascended the staircase and went to bed. It was all a grand illusion, specially prepared for spying eyes. But after the lights were turned out, there would be no sleep — only waiting to see if the plan would work.

My head itched under the fancy wig. And the girdle was too tight — I could hardly breathe. The false eyelashes irritated my eyes. No, it was not Fifi who waited alone in the bedroom but an imposter, I am sorry to say, named Ralph Miller.

The grand lady was hidden in another room. The

butler, who kept repeating, "This cops and robbers business is getting out of hand" had gone straight to his room and bolted the doors and windows. Bruno and Daschell were hidden somewhere in the shadows — ready for action.

The house was quiet, too quiet, I thought. Then suddenly someone turned on the stereo full blast. The walls began shaking from top to bottom. "I'll be down to get you in a taxi, honey," the singer croaked, "better be ready 'bout a half past eight."

I jumped out of bed and ran into the hallway but before I could call out for Daschell and Bruno, I was trapped in a padded box and the lid locked shut.

I couldn't see anything — but I could smell the faint odor of cigar smoke and onions.

The plan was working all right. But *whose* plan, I wondered. Was it Daschell's or had the plan of the Boss just taken over?

13

OPERATION PAC-MAN

As the box in which I was held captive was carried from the house, I listened for the sound of the mysterious black sedan. Instead, I heard the noise of another type of engine. It made a whop, whop, whop type of racket. What on earth? I wondered. Then, I realized that it didn't come from anything on earth but from something hovering in the sky — a helicopter! We hadn't expected that.

Up to this point, I hadn't even been afraid. But

now, I knew we — *we?* — **I** was in real trouble. How could Daschell and Bruno follow a helicopter? They couldn't. So much for Daschell's master plan.

Other than the rumbling sound that the helicopter made as it lifted off, I had the feeling of "deja vu" and rightfully so. I had experienced all of this before — trapped in a box, the smell of cigar smoke and onions, being whisked off to some unknown destination. "Well, Ralph," I told myself. "You never learn. You've done it again."

In less than an hour, I could feel the helicopter beginning to descend and, finally, it touched down. The box I was in was quickly picked up and carried away from the noise. As the box jolted from side to side, I realized I was being carried up a flight of stairs. I could hear the heavy footsteps of my captors. A door was opened and then shut. Then, there was another flight of stairs and, finally, the box was dropped to the floor.

"Open the box," I heard a voice say. I knew who said it. I had heard that voice before. It was the voice of the Boss.

A key was inserted into the lock and turned. Then, the lid was opened.

"Well, well, well," the Boss said with a smirk. "What have we here?"

The fat one looked down at the ribbon on the wig I was wearing.

"Looks like we got a sissy dog," he said.

"Watch your mouth, fat stuff," I warned.

"What a big voice you have, Miss Fifi," the Boss said mockingly.

"I'm not Fifi," I declared, quickly pulling off the wig and removing the eyelashes. "Guess we fooled you this time."

"Not quite, Mr. Miller," the Boss said. "We were onto your game from the beginning."

"Says you," I replied, not able to think of a better retort.

"Yes," he said, "says I," reaching out and pushing the buzzer on the wall.

The side door opened and there stood the butler, holding Fifi, bound and gagged. She struggled to get loose but the ropes held her tight.

"Shall I put the little monster in the hole?" the butler inquired.

"Yes," the Boss agreed.

The butler carried Fifi from the room and the door was shut.

"I might have known the butler did it," I said with disgust.

"Every man has his price," the Boss informed me.

The fat one relit his cigar and the skinny one stood there twirling his silly lasso.

"You may be in for a couple of surprises yet," I said with forced bravery.

The fat one laughed and the skinny one snickered.

"If you are referring to your friend, Bruno, and that has-been detective, Daschell," the Boss replied, "I'm afraid you're in for a very long wait. The last we saw of them, they were locked in boxes similar to yours and placed on a skyjacked plane to Cuba. My friend, Fidel, knows how to deal with their kind."

"You louse," I said with disgust.

"Your choice of words is disappointing," the Boss said, "especially coming from a published author. Oh, yes, I've read your book. It's quite impressive."

"I hate to think of the likes of you even buying a copy," I sneered.

"Oh, I didn't buy it," he replied. "I read the original manuscript."

"The original manuscript? But how?"

"If you had bothered to research publishers better," he said, "you might have learned who owns Apex Publishing Company."

"You!" I exclaimed, finally understanding it all. What a fool I had been.

"And the Tonight Show?" I asked.

"It was easy to arrange," the Boss replied. "I own the major stock in NBC, CBS, and ABC and most of the cable networks as well."

"And all from the Bubble Gum Caper?" I asked.

"Why, yes," he chuckled. "I see you've tied all the strings together. How very clever of you, Ralph. The great Bubble Gum Caper began it all. That's why I wanted you."

"Me?" I replied. "I thought you wanted Fifi."

"I want you both," he said. "Fifi is no more than a mere object to look at — like a statue or a painting. But you have intellect — you can think and respond to genius."

"You have the fat one and the skinny one," I reminded him.

"They are nothing but dummies who do as I tell them."

"But Boss . . ." the skinny one groaned.

"Shut up!" the Boss ordered. "If it weren't for me, you and your sidekick would be cooling your heels in some prison cell."

The fat one grumbled something under his breath and the skinny one twirled his lasso nervously.

"Do you see what I mean?" the Boss said to me. "They are nothing but stooges. They can't possibly appreciate genius such as mine."

"And what about Josie?" I asked.

"Nothing," he shrugged. "She's yours if you want her."

"Josie isn't some object you can take or give away," I insisted. "She's a person."

"Not according to the law," he replied.

He had me there.

"Don't look so forlorn, Ralph," the Boss said. "Life will be very pleasant for us all. You may write as many books as you like and I will see that they are published. You will have Josie for company. And I can show you my future plans. It will be a fascinating life."

"What plans?" I questioned.

"Do you see what I mean?" he said to the fat one and the skinny one. "You see how quick he is? The

The Boss —
He's got to be stopped.

mere mention of plans and he wants to know. The both of you stand there like the dummies you are. But not Ralph. He has something you'll never have — he has curiosity."

The Boss reached forward and pressed a button on the table. The wall behind him began to move. As it opened, I could see an enormous control panel that stretched across the room.

"Okay," I said, "I'm impressed."

"Wait until you hear the plan," he laughed. "It will curl your hair. It is called — Operation Pac-Man!"

"What?"

"Operation Pac-Man," he repeated. "If you think the Bubble Gum Caper was something, wait till you hear this. The bubble gum craze is over, right? Today, the children of the world have a new addiction."

"Video games!" I exclaimed.

"And who do you think owns all the video games companies?" he asked.

"You do," I concluded.

"Exactly," he replied. "And what you see before you is my own invention. At precisely midnight tonight, the control panel will activate three satellites that are now circling the globe and, in seconds, the video games — the world over— will be demagnetized!"

"What a diabolical scheme," I said, shaking my head.

"Yes," he laughed wildly. "Can you imagine the panic tomorrow morning? The little tykes will get out of bed, run to their TV sets and turn on their plastic control panels and the screens will go haywire — all programs will be blank. By midmorning, the children will be driving their parents crazy. All businesses will stop, governments will be destroyed, nations will crumble. I will control the world!"

"You are insane," I told him.

He suddenly stopped and looked at the fat one and the skinny one.

"Put him in Cell Block Two," he ordered.

Before I could move, I was grabbed up by the fat one and the skinny one and carried down the steps and locked in a concrete cell. There was no way to escape and Operation Pac-Man was set into motion.

THE FINAL COUNTDOWN

The hours passed slowly. When I heard voices in the hallway, I pressed my ear to the door.

"He had no right to call us dummies," I heard the skinny one whine.

"Forget it," the fat one gruffed.

"But we got feelings, too," the skinny one insisted.

I could hear them open a door down the hall.

"Here, eat this," the fat one said.

They must have given food to another captive. Perhaps, to Fifi — or even Josie. Then, I heard a "yip, yip, yip" and I knew it was Fifi.

When a key was turned in the lock of my door, I prepared for action. But the minute the door was opened, the fat one's foot sent me hurtling into the corner. And the skinny one laughed.

Then, suddenly, both men were thrown forward. The fat one hit against the wall with a deafening thud and the skinny one was thrown upside down.

"How do you like them apples, fatso?" I heard a voice say.

"Daschell!" I said. "I thought you were in Cuba."

After he gave another chop to the back of the fat one's neck, Daschell's foot pinned the skinny one flat to the floor.

"Didn't care much for that idea," he replied.

"Are you all right, Ralph?" Bruno asked, entering the cell.

"I am now."

At Daschell's instructions, we tied the hands of the skinny one and the fat one behind their backs.

I quickly told Daschell about Operation Pac-Man.

"It's six minutes till midnight," he said. "That doesn't give us much time."

"We called the police," Bruno said. "They're on the way."

"They won't be here in time," Daschell replied. "We've got to stop the Boss without them."

"Yes," I agreed. "The lives and happiness of millions of children are in our paws."

We unlocked the other cell and let Fifi out. Daschell told her to do exactly as he instructed. After we made our way up the darkened staircase, Fifi was stationed at the front door of the control room while Daschell, Bruno, and I edged quietly down the hallway until we reached the back door. We could hear the Boss call out, "Eddie" and "Charlie" and then grumble, "Where are those idiots?"

At Daschell's signal, Fifi started barking, "Yip, yip, yip." When we heard the Boss hurry toward the front door, Daschell, Bruno, and I rushed inside, positioning ourselves between the Boss and the control panel.

"So," Daschell said to the Boss. "We meet at last."

The Boss turned around. Deciding to make a run

for it, he opened the front door and was he ever surprised! Fifi jumped at him like a tigress, barking and biting, forcing him to his knees.

"Call her off," he pleaded.

Although Daschell did — you know Fifi. She didn't stop until she was good and ready. She nipped his heels and tore his shirt and pants to ribbons. Bruno and I had to pull her off him.

We looked at the clock. Only two minutes to zero!

Daschell turned toward the Boss. "Turn it off!" he demanded.

"I'll make you rich," the Boss replied, trying to get his breath. "You'll make more money than you ever dreamed of."

"Turn it off!" Daschell insisted.

"But we can control the world!" Boss exclaimed.

"Turn it off!"

"I can't," the Boss whined. "I won't."

"Then, you won't live to enjoy it," Daschell told him. "Fifi, he's all yours."

Miss Fifi licked her lips and bared her teeth. She growled a low, menacing sound and started moving toward the Boss.

"No, no," the Boss screamed. "I'll tell you how."

"Halt!" Daschell commanded.

"Let me take just one more bite," Fifi scowled.

"No," the Boss screamed again. "All you have to do is pull the plug."

"Where is it?" I asked.

"On the wall over there," the Boss pointed.

With no time to spare, I ran to the wall, grabbed the plug with both paws and yanked it out of the socket. The lights on the control panel flickered and dimmed and the discs stopped spinning. I looked up at the clock — ten seconds to zero!

Two more no's and one more bite and it would have been too late.

"Better call Fifi off," I said to Daschell.

"You do it," Daschell replied. "That dame scares me to death."

When Fifi growled again, we agreed to let her guard the Boss until the police arrived.

"Wait a minute — Josie," I suddenly remembered. "Where's Josie?"

"She was locked in the kennel outside," Bruno said. "Daschell and I released her before we came in. I think you will find her waiting by the gate."

I ran to the front porch.

"Ralph," I heard her voice call and saw her

running toward the house.

"Oh, Josie," I cried and jumped off the porch and ran to meet her.

"How wonderful," Bruno said, standing by the window.

"Yeh," Daschell replied, "but spare me all that drippy stuff."

"Let me take just one more bite before the cops get here," Fifi pleaded.

"No!" cried the Boss.

I'll never know if they let Fifi have one last and final bite or not. But if she really wanted to, I don't think Daschell and Bruno were big enough or strong enough to have stopped her.

Don't you like stories with happy endings? I do. And ours has more than one.

The Boss and his sidekicks — the fat one and the skinny one — were sent to prison.

As you probably guessed, Fifi was launched as a star and was signed by a major Hollywood studio to make the film, "Forever Fifi" — costarring Burt Reynolds, Elizabeth Taylor, and Sir Laurence Olivier.

Daschell had cracked the biggest case of his career.

And Bruno, my loyal and trustworthy friend, was allowed to sleep away the mornings and afternoons as he pleased.

As for me — well, due to the headline coverage, my book skyrocketed to the top of the best seller list. And of course, the best part of all, Josie and I were together again, and we were free and safe — or so I thought.

Last night, the telephone rang and when Jeff answered, a very high, squeaky voice said, "Tell that dog he'll be mine before the week is out."

Jeff thought someone was just playing a prank — but I don't know.

If you happen to see a mysterious black sedan or a purple station wagon or a pink truck in your neighborhood, write down the number of the license plate and call the police!

Until we meet again, I remain yours very truly,

Ralph Miller

David Melton —author and illustrator

David Melton is one of the most versatile and prolific talents on the literary and art scenes today. His literary works span the gamut of factual prose, analytical essays, newsreporting, magazine articles, features, short stories, poetry and novels in both the adult and juvenile fields. When reviewing his credits, it is difficult to believe that such an outpouring of creative efforts came from just one person. In seventeen years, twenty-four of his books have been published, several of which have been translated into a number of languages.

Mr. Melton has illustrated ten of his own books and three by other authors, while many of his drawings and paintings have been reproduced as fine art prints, posters, puzzles, calendars, book jackets, record covers, mobiles and note cards, and they have been featured in national publications.

Mr. Melton has also gained wide reputation as a guest speaker and teacher. He has spoken to hundreds of professional, social and civic groups, relating the problems that confront parents and teachers of learning-disabled and handicapped children, and he has influenced the mandates of change in the field of special education and therapies for brain-injured children. He is also a frequent guest on local and national radio and television talk shows.

Since a number of Mr. Melton's books are enjoyed by children, he has visited hundreds of schools nationwide as a principal speaker in Author-in-Residence Programs, Young Authors' Days, and Children's Literature Festivals. He also conducts in-service seminars for teachers and teaches professional writing courses throughout the country.

To encourage and celebrate the creativity of students, Mr. Melton has developed the highly acclaimed teacher's manual, WRITTEN & ILLUSTRATED BY..., which is used in thousands of schools in teaching students to write and illustrate original books by *THE MELTON METHOD*. To provide opportunities for students to become professionally published authors and illustrators, in association with Landmark Editions, Inc., he helped initiate THE NATIONAL WRITTEN & ILLUSTRATED BY... AWARDS CONTEST FOR STUDENTS.

OTHER BOOKS BY DAVID MELTON

Author:
TODD   *Prentice Hall* (Softcover, *Dell*)
New Edition — *The Better Baby Press*
WHEN CHILDREN NEED HELP   *T. Y. Crowell*
CHILDREN OF DREAMS, CHILDREN OF HOPE   *Contemporary Books*
New Edition — *The Better Baby Press*
A BOY CALLED HOPELESS   *Independence Press*
(Softcover, Scholastic Press)
New Edition — *Landmark Editions*
THEODORE   *Independence Press*
SURVIVAL KIT FOR PARENTS OF TEENAGERS   *St. Martin's Press*
PROMISES TO KEEP   *Franklin Watts*
WRITTEN & ILLUSTRATED BY...   *Landmark Editions*

Author and Illustrator:
I'LL SHOW YOU THE MORNING SUN   *Stanyan-Random House*
JUDY — A REMEMBRANCE   *Stanyan-Random House*
THIS MAN, JESUS   *McGraw Hill*
AND GOD CREATED...   *Independence Press*
HOW TO HELP YOUR PRESCHOOLER LEARN MORE, FASTER AND
BETTER   *David McKay*
THE ONE AND ONLY AUTOBIOGRAPHY OF RALPH MILLER —
The Dog Who Knew He Was a Boy   *Independence Press*
New Edition — *Landmark Editions*
HARRY S. TRUMAN — THE MAN WHO WALKED WITH GIANTS
Independence Press
HOW TO CAPTURE LIVE AUTHORS AND BRING THEM TO YOUR
SCHOOLS
Landmark Editions
INDEPENDENCE — THE QUEEN CITY OF THE TRAILS
Landmark Editions

Illustrator:
WHAT TO DO ABOUT YOUR BRAIN-INJURED CHILD
by Glenn Doman   *Doubleday*
GOOD-BYE, MOMMY
by Bruce King Doman
The Better Baby Press and *Encyclopaedia Britannica*
IMAGES OF GREATNESS
Independence Press and *Images of Greatness Commission*
HOW TO BE YOUR OWN ASTROLOGER
by Sybil Leek   *Cowles Book Co.*

Editor and Designer:
HAPPY BIRTHDAY, AMERICA!   *Independence Press*

If You Haven't Read

You've Missed Half the Fun!

Now published by

LANDMARK EDITIONS

1420 Kansas Avenue
Kansas City, Missouri 64127

A DAVID MELTON NOVEL

There was something wrong with Jeremiah Rodgers. That *something* would change the lives of those in his family, because that something was SOMETHING TERRIBLE!

"Tender, heartwarming and courageous, with moments of high drama. This is a book young and old will read with admiration and empathy."
— **Committee of the Elementary School Booklist of the National Council of Teachers of English**

Now published by

LANDMARK EDITIONS

1420 Kansas Avenue
Kansas City, Missouri 64127